BLOOD WHEELS

Titles in Full Flight 6

Hard Drive Boy	Jonny Zucker
Robot Safe Crackers	Jonny Zucker
Blood Wheels	Stan Cullimore
Surf Attack	Alison Hawes
The Dream Catcher	Jane A.C. West
Framed!	Jillian Powell
House of Fear	Tony Norman
Go-Kart Crazy	Roger Hurn
Spirit Tribe	Melanie Joyce
Lunar Rover	David Orme

Badger Publishing Limited
15 Wedgwood Gate, Pin Green Industrial Estate,
Stevenage, Hertfordshire SG1 4SU
Telephone: 01438 356907. Fax: 01438 747015.
www.badger-publishing.co.uk
enquiries@badger-publishing.co.uk

Blood Wheels ISBN 978-1-84691-663-2

Series Editor: Jonny Zucker
Publisher: David Jamieson.
Editor: Danny Pearson
Design: Fi Grant
Cover illustration: Paul Savage

Blood Wheels

Contents

Badger Publishing

Chapter 1
It Followed Me

Jack was eating his breakfast when his mobile phone began to ring. It was his friend Eve.

"Hi, Jack," said Eve. "Do you want to hang out in the park?"

"Good idea," said Jack. "Let me finish my breakfast and I'll meet you."

“Where?”

“At the end of the road,” said Jack.

Ten minutes later, Jack was sitting on the wall at the end of the road. Next to a STOP sign.

Eve came running up. She stopped in front of him and looked about. As if she was scared of something.

“Are you OK?” asked Jack.

Eve shook her head. “Not really.” She looked as if she had been running very fast.

“Have you been running?”

Eve nodded and looked over her shoulder. “Yes.”

“Why?” asked Jack. He could see that Eve was shaking.

Eve gulped. “There was this car. It was really - odd.”

“What do you mean, odd?”

“Well, for a start it had big yellow flames painted down the sides.”

Jack nodded. “Sounds cool.”

“And it followed me,” said Eve.

“What do you mean, it followed you?”

“I mean that it drove along the road, really slowly. Following me.”

Jack laughed. “Eve, you were walking along the road. Cars drive along the road. It wasn't following you. It was just doing what cars do!”

He jumped off the wall and held out his hands. As if he was holding the steering wheel of a car. “Come on. You lead the way to the park. I'll follow you.”

Chapter 2
It's Going To Hit Us!

“It's not funny, Jack,” said Eve. “It almost knocked me down.”

Jack kept on going along the road. He turned the corner.

“Jack!” shouted Eve. “Where are you going?”

Jack came back round the corner.

“What colour was that car?” he asked.

“It was red,” replied Eve.

Jack pulled a face. “Then it's waiting for you round the corner.”

Eve took hold of Jack’s arm. “Are you serious?” She looked at him.

Jack nodded. Eve looked back the way they had just come. “Come on,” she said. “We'll go to the park another way.”

Jack looked as if he was going to say something. But then he stopped himself. He nodded. "I'm not scared," he said slowly. "But if you are, we'll go another way."

The two friends turned and walked back along the road. They came to another road going up hill. They began to walk along it.

"What was that?" asked Eve as they walked past an advert for Chewing Gum.

"What?" asked Jack. He was in a bit of a bad mood. He didn't really want to run away from a stupid car!

"I heard something," said Eve.

"Well, I didn't," said Jack. "You're just making things up now."

At that moment, the red car with flames on the side skidded round the corner in front of them. It stopped in the middle of the road. The engine roared. Then the car shot forward, heading right at Jack and Eve.

"It's going to hit us!" shouted Eve.

Jack grabbed his friend and pulled them both into a bush.

The car shot past - going very fast.

Chapter 3
It's Ok, We've Lost It

Jack jumped up out of the bush.

"The driver of that car is an idiot!" he shouted. "He could have knocked us down."

"I think he was trying to knock us down," said Eve.

Jack looked at her. "Why would he want to do that?"

Eve shrugged. "I don't know. But like I said before. There is something really odd about that car."

"Well, there is no time to think about that now," said Jack.

"He's coming back. Come on, let's get out of here."

Eve looked along the road. The red car had turned round and was coming back towards them again.

"Follow me," hissed Jack.

He took Eve by the hand and pulled her into a little back lane. They ran along it as it twisted and turned past lots of old sheds.

“I never even knew about this little lane,” said Eve.

“No-one really uses it anymore,” said Jack. “It goes right behind the houses and comes out by the park.”

Soon the two friends were in the park. There was a road along one side, then a patch of grass. There was a high fence beside the grass.

On the other side of the fence there was a long drop called 'The Sea Wall.' There were signs on the fence saying;
'Danger. Keep Away.'

"It's ok, we've lost it," said Jack.

"No, we haven't," said Eve sadly.

She pointed. The car was driving over the grass. Heading right at them.

"How did it find us?" gasped Jack.

Eve shrugged. "I don't know. But I don't think it's going to leave us alone ... until it's got our blood on its wheels."

Jack looked grim. "Are you OK to run for a bit, Eve?"

She nodded. Jack looked at her. He looked very serious.

"I've got an idea," he said. "But you must do exactly what I say. Can you do that?"

Eve nodded again.

Jack pointed at a tree at the other side of the park.

"You need to run over to that tree. I want the car to follow you."

Eve gasped. "What if it gets me?"

"It won't get you. It will be trying to get me,"

Jack pulled a face. “But don’t worry. It’s a trap!”

He smiled grimly.

“Now, when you get to the tree I want you to start waving at the car and shouting.”

Eve looked surprised.

“No more talking,” said Jack.
“Get ready to run when I count to three. One, two, three.”

Eve ran over to the tree.

Jack stepped out in front of the car. He threw out his arms.

"Hey, you! Idiot in the car. Catch me if you can."

Chapter 5
That's Not Good At All

The car engine roared. The car shot forward heading right at Jack. At the last moment Jack jumped to the side.

The car shot past him. Then, with a loud roar, it skidded to a stop.

Eve stopped running. "Look out, Jack!" she cried.

"Keep on running, Eve," shouted Jack.

"Do what I told you, please, Eve!"

Jack turned back to look at the car.

The engine roared and the car shot forward again.

But this time, Jack didn't move out of the way.

He waited until the car was almost on top of him. Then, suddenly, he bent down and grabbed the door handle.

He pulled open the door and jumped inside the car.

"I don't know who you are," he shouted as he fell on the seat. "But you are being an idiot. You could have knocked us ...."

He stopped. The car was empty. There was nobody in the driving seat.

"This is bad news," said Jack.
"I'm getting out of here."

He pulled on the door handle. But nothing moved. The door was shut and it would not open.

"This is really bad news," said Jack.

Chapter 6
Change Of Plan

He looked up and saw Eve. She was standing by the tree and waving at the car.

"Oh no," said Jack.

"She's doing what I told her to do. But there is no driver in the car. Now what can I do?"

He tried to open the door, but it would not move.

"Time for a change of plan," said Jack.

He thought, fast. Then, he looked at the sign above Eve. It read; Danger. Sea Wall. This Way.

Jack smiled. “It has to work,” he thought to himself.

“Hey, you car,” he said out loud.

“If you drive really fast at Eve you will be able to get her. That’s what you want, isn’t it? Blood on your wheels.”

The car engine roared. The car raced over the grass towards Eve. Jack opened the window.

“Eve,” he shouted. “Jump behind the tree!”

Eve jumped behind the tree as the car shot past her. A second later, Jack jumped out of the window of the car.

There was a loud BANG as the car hit the high fence. Then the car was through the fence and was falling down, down - all the way.

It didn’t stop falling until it got to the bottom of the Sea Wall.

“We’ve done it,” cried Jack. “We’re safe!”

Eve jumped at him and the two friends hugged.

Jack smiled. “Eve, next time you want to hang out in the park. Try not to get followed by a crazy car.”

Eve laughed. “Good idea.”

Down below and far away a headlight twinkled into life.

Then there came the sound of a car engine.

But Jack and Eve did not hear it... yet.